Cambridge Experience Readers

Level 2

Series editor: Nicholas Ti*

As Others See Us

Nicola Prentis

CAMBRIDGE
UNIVERSITY PRESS

CAMBRIDGE
UNIVERSITY PRESS

University Printing House, Cambridge CB2 8BS, United Kingdom

Cambridge University Press is part of the University of Cambridge.

It furthers the University's mission by disseminating knowledge in the pursuit of education, learning and research at the highest international levels of excellence.

www.cambridge.org
Information on this title: www.cambridge.org/9781107699199

First published 2014

Nicola Prentis has asserted her right to be identified as the Author of the Work in accordance with the Copyright, Design and Patents Act 1988.

Printed In Italy by Rotolito Lombardo S.p.A

ISBN 978-1107-699-19-9 Paperback

Illustrations by Lance Tooks

Audio recording by BraveArts

Cover image by Getty Images/Mark Mawson

Typeset by Óscar Latorre

Contents

People in the story

Gemma: a fifteen-year-old schoolgirl
Mum: Gemma's mother
Shop assistant: an old man who works in a phone shop
Amy: Gemma's best friend
Robert: the best-looking boy in school
Mrs Hawkins: Gemma and Amy's music teacher at school

BEFORE YOU READ

1 Look at the pictures in Chapter 1. Answer the questions.

 1 What do Gemma and her mum want to buy?

 2 What is special about Gemma's new phone?

It's not fair!

'But Mum, I need *this* one!' Gemma said. She pulled her mother's arm and pointed at the phone.

'You *need* new shoes and a winter coat, Gemma. You don't *need* the most expensive phone in the shop,' her mother said. She was tired of having the same conversation for ten minutes.

'You don't understand!' said Gemma. Everyone at school has this one. I want a cool phone too! If I wear last year's winter coat, can I have it?'

'How many times do I have to say "no"? It's good to be different sometimes.'

'I don't want to be different!' argued Gemma. 'I've seen your photos from when you were fifteen. Your clothes were the same as your friends'. They looked stupid, but they were cool then, weren't they?' Now her mother had to agree.

'First, none of my clothes were as expensive as this phone. Second, you're right, they did look stupid. People can sometimes look very stupid when they're trying to be cool.'

'But *please* Mum! I never get anything I want.'

'No, Gemma. You can have any of the phones on this side of the shop or we go home right now. I'll find someone to help you.' She went to find the shop assistant.

Gemma pretended[1] to look at the phones. She wasn't really looking, she was too angry. She didn't want one of those phones. They weren't much better than her old phone. Her mother was so unfair!

'Do you see what you're looking for?' asked a voice in her ear.

She turned round to find a strange-looking old man behind her. He was quite short, only as tall as Gemma, and he had light green eyes and a friendly, smiling face.

'I …' Gemma started. She didn't know what to say. She *could* see what she wanted, but she couldn't have it. 'Do you work here?' she asked.

'Yes, I do and maybe we have something you'll like,' he said. 'Your friends all have those phones, don't they?' He pointed to the phones on the other side of the shop.

'Yes,' said Gemma. 'But it's not fair. Mum says I can't have one of those.'

'Mums don't always understand these things,' the old man said. 'Let's show your mum something special.'

Gemma went with him to the back of the shop. Gemma's mother followed them. The man took out a box. 'Now this is the new—' he started to say.

'I'm sorry,' said Gemma's mother. 'I've told Gemma we can't buy this kind of phone. It's too expensive.'

'But this one is free,' the old man said quickly.

Gemma's mouth opened, but she couldn't speak. Her mother looked very surprised[2], too.

'Free?' Gemma asked.

'What?' asked her mother.

'Well, it's almost free,' the shop assistant said. 'There is something—'

'I knew it was too good to be true, Gemma,' said her mum quickly.

'Oh,' said Gemma. The smile left her face.

'Do we have to pay every month?' her mother asked. 'But that won't make it cheaper. I'm sure it's still too expensive.'

'As I was saying,' the old man said, 'this is new, so there are only a few in the country. It is very special, but it hasn't been tested yet. The phone makers want to know what people think about it. Gemma can have it for free, but she has to come back in two weeks and tell me about it. Then I can write a report[3] for the phone makers.'

'What special things can it do?' asked Gemma.

'Oh, you'll see,' the old man said.

'Can I have it, Mum? Please!'

'I can't say "no" now, can I?' her mother answered, but she didn't look as excited as Gemma. 'But I'm not very happy about it. What if you lose it? I'm sure it's an expensive phone and maybe we'll have to pay for it.'

'Don't worry,' said the shop assistant to Gemma's mother. 'If she loses it, I can find it again.'

Gemma was only half listening.

'Everyone at school will be jealous[4] of me. They'll all want one too,' she said.

'They'll probably all want to try it, Gemma,' the old man told her. 'But you mustn't lend it to anyone. It's only for you.'

'OK.' Gemma didn't care about that. 'Can I have it, Mum? Please?'

Gemma's mother couldn't think how to say 'no' again, so she agreed. The man took the phone out of its box and showed it to Gemma. It was made out of something strange that changed colour when it moved. It was as light as air and very thin. Gemma loved it.

She didn't stop looking at it all the way to the car. She turned it on and it changed from grey to red. That was cool, but the next thing it did was a bigger surprise[5].

On the screen was some text.

'How does it know my name?' she thought. 'The man in the shop didn't put my name in it. I was watching him.'

The screen changed again. 'Gemma? Ready?'

She pushed 'OK'.

Chapter 2

It's amazing!

When they got home, Gemma ran to her room to try out her new phone. At first, she was really happy to have a great phone like everyone else at school. But after playing with it for a while, she was bored. It changed colours and knew her name, but that was all that was different from her old phone. She looked and looked, but she couldn't find anything else special about it.

'But if the phone isn't special, why does the man want me to give him a report?' she thought.

* * *

The next morning Gemma decided not to tell anyone, even her best friend Amy, about the man in the shop. She couldn't say how her phone was different, so it was better to say nothing. When she arrived at school, everyone was sending messages on their phones. She took out hers to do the same thing.

'Cool!' said Amy. 'When did you get that new phone? It's amazing⁶!'

'Yesterday. But—' Gemma started.

'Let me see,' said another girl. She pushed Amy out of the way so she could see better. 'Where did you get that?'

'It's new—' Gemma started again.

'We can see that,' said Amy. 'Where did you get it? I've never seen a phone like it.'

They weren't listening any more. Amy took the phone

from Gemma. Then everyone was shouting and fighting to try it. Soon some boys came and there were lots of people and Gemma was pushed to the back. She didn't understand what everyone else could see. Then she remembered what the old man said about not giving the phone to anyone. She pushed to the front again.

'Look!' said one of the boys.

'How did it do that?' asked Amy. She pointed to the screen. Gemma took the phone back and looked at it. It said:

'This is Gemma's phone. Please give me back to her. Where is Gemma?'

Just then, they heard the bell for the first lesson. So Gemma didn't need to answer Amy's question. When they went into school, people were talking about the phone. Some of them were trying to walk close to Gemma to look. She put it in her pocket so they couldn't see it.

'Your hair's different today, Gemma,' Amy said. 'It looks really good. I think I'm going to do mine the same way. Can you show me how?'

Gemma didn't know what Amy was talking about. Her hair was the same as every day – boring and tied back in a ponytail.

'And,' Amy said, 'I love your new shoes. Your mum bought you a phone and shoes! Lucky you!'

Now Gemma really didn't understand. Her shoes weren't new at all. They were just her old school shoes.

'These shoes? They're nothing special. What do you mean?' asked Gemma.

Amy laughed.

'You're joking, Gemma! Nothing special? I've seen them in magazines. They're really cool! Wait a minute! Have you got a new bag too?'

'This?' said Gemma. She pointed at her school bag. It was dirty and it looked old. 'No! What are you talking about?'

'It's beautiful. I'm so jealous!' said Amy.

Gemma was more than surprised – she didn't know what she was feeling. As they walked to class, she could see that most of the girls were looking at her. Their eyes moved from her hair to her bag and down to her shoes. It was like they saw something special too.

What was happening?

LOOKING BACK

1 Check your answers to *Before you read* on page 4.

ACTIVITIES

2 Complete the sentences with the names in the box.

> the old man (x2) Gemma (x2) Mum Amy (x2)

1 *Gemma* wants a cool new phone.
2 .... doesn't want to buy an expensive new phone.
3 .... has to tell .... about the phone after two weeks.
4 .... has to write a report for the phone makers.
5 .... can find the phone if it gets lost.
6 .... takes Gemma's phone from her at school.
7 .... likes Gemma's hair.

3 Are the sentences true (*T*) or false (*F*)?

1 Gemma wants the same kind of phone as her friends. ☐ *T*
2 Gemma's new phone doesn't cost anything. ☐
3 The new phone changes colour. ☐
4 The old man puts Gemma's name into the phone. ☐
5 The new phone knows Gemma's name. ☐
6 Gemma has got a new bag. ☐

4 Underline the correct words in each sentence.

1 Gemma *wants* / *needs* the most expensive phone in the shop.

2 Gemma wants to be *different from* / *like* her friends.

3 The old man in the shop is *friendly* / *unfriendly*.

4 Gemma thinks *everyone* / *no one* at school will want a phone like hers.

5 Gemma *can* / *can't* find lots of special things about the phone.

6 Gemma *wants* / *doesn't want* to tell Amy about the phone.

7 At school, Gemma puts the phone in her *pocket* / *bag*.

8 Gemma's shoes are *old* / *new*.

5 Answer the questions.

1 Why is Gemma angry with her mum in the shop?

....

2 Why are Gemma and her mum surprised about the new phone?

....

3 Why does Gemma get bored with her new phone?

....

4 Why does everyone want to see Gemma's phone?

....

LOOKING FORWARD

6 Tick (✓) the things you think are true in the next two chapters.

1 Gemma works really hard at school. ☐

2 Gemma makes a new friend. ☐

15

Chapter 3

That's strange!

Their first lesson was history. Everyone was still talking about Gemma. She could hear them. Even when the teacher arrived, they didn't stop.

'Quiet!' said the teacher, but no one stopped talking. 'I said quiet!' he shouted again. 'I hope everyone did their homework because we're going to start with a short test.'

Now it was quiet. Everyone was listening.

Gemma looked at Amy and made a face. They were like each other in a lot of ways. They both loved music, but they weren't very good in their other classes. Perhaps that was why they were best friends.

Amy's mouth made the words 'I forgot about the homework.'

'Me too!' replied Gemma.

'Question one,' the teacher started. 'Which street did the Great Fire of London start in?'

Gemma wasn't very good at history. There was too much to remember and she wasn't interested in things that happened long ago. She wrote the first thing that came into her head for each question. But she knew most of the answers were wrong. Out of twenty questions, she thought five of them were right. At the end, she gave her paper to Amy. The teacher read out the answers and they checked each other's papers.

Amy gave Gemma her paper back and smiled. 'Wow, Gemma!' she said quietly, so the teacher couldn't hear. 'You *did* do your homework. But why did you say you forgot?'

Gemma looked at her paper. Twenty out of twenty correct. She couldn't understand it. She turned to Amy.

'Why did you give me twenty? The teacher is going to be angry with both of us.'

'But you got them all right,' Amy said. She looked at her paper. 'I only got six right.'

'Is there a problem, Gemma?' the teacher asked.

'Amy didn't check my test correctly. I was just asking her,' said Gemma.

The teacher took Gemma's paper and read the answers quickly. 'Wow! Twenty out of twenty. That's a lovely surprise, Gemma. Well done!'

Some people in the class clapped[7].

'Go, Gemma!' shouted one of the boys.

Gemma didn't know what to say. She felt her face go red. She couldn't argue with the teacher, but she knew some of her answers were wrong. Perhaps he was trying to be kind because she didn't do well. But that wasn't like him. It wasn't like any teacher.

'Perhaps he's going to talk to me about it after the class,' she thought. She worried about it for the rest of the lesson, but the teacher didn't ask to see her at the end.

* * *

The afternoon was as strange as the morning. Now it wasn't only the people in Gemma's class who wanted to see the phone. Older students she didn't know were coming and asking to look at it.

'It's really cool, Gemma,' said one older girl.

'Tell us how you got it!' said another girl.

'It's not a big story really,' said Gemma. 'It's just a new phone. A man in the shop said I could try it for two weeks. Then I have to tell him what I think of it.'

'That's so exciting!' the girl said. 'What an amazing story!'

'What?' Gemma thought. To her surprise, more and more people came to listen. So she told them about the old man and the phone too. They asked her to tell the story again and again. Soon, everyone knew who Gemma was. She felt like someone famous. She was the coolest person in school. She stopped thinking that the story was nothing special. It was special to everyone else and that was enough.

*   *   *

'How was school?' asked her mother when she came home from work.

'OK,' said Gemma. 'But a bit strange—'

'Yes, your history teacher emailed me today. He told me what you got in the test.'

'Oh no!' Gemma thought. She knew there was something strange about that test. But why didn't the teacher talk to her about it? Why did he email her mother? Now she had a big problem!

'I don't know what happened. I don't know why I did so well in the test,' said Gemma.

Her mother wasn't listening.

'It's wonderful that you're doing so well in school. All your teachers are really happy with you. And I am too!'

Gemma didn't know what to say.

'Thanks. I think I'm going to go to my room and do my homework.'

Her mother smiled. 'That's why you're so good in school!'

Gemma went to her room. She had a maths test the next day, and she wanted to study. But first she watched some TV. Then she looked at her maths book for ten minutes before dinner. After dinner, there was a good film on TV, so she watched that. Soon it was too late to study.

'I can study tomorrow morning,' she thought as she went to sleep.

*   *   *

In the morning, Gemma looked at her maths book while she was eating breakfast. It wasn't enough time. She was afraid when she went to her maths class and did the test. But when she got her paper back she had an A.

'Well done, Gemma!' said her teacher.

'Again? You said you didn't study!' said Amy.

'I only looked at my book for a few minutes!' Gemma said.

'You're just much cleverer than me,' said Amy.

Gemma didn't know what to say. She didn't know why she was suddenly[8] doing so well at school.

'Someone is going to ask me why sooner or later. What am I going to say?' she thought.

Chapter 4

What happened to the teacher?

In the afternoon they had a tennis lesson. Gemma put her phone into her pocket. She didn't want anyone to look at it while she was playing.

Gemma liked tennis, but she wasn't very good at it. She played with Amy while the teacher watched.

'Very good, Gemma,' the teacher said when Gemma hit[9] the ball to Amy. But the ball was out.

'No, it was out!' Gemma told her teacher.

'No, no. It was in,' said Amy. '15–0.'

Gemma hit the ball to Amy again. She thought it was out again, but no one said anything. Amy couldn't hit it back, so it was 30–0 to Gemma. Then Gemma hit the ball into the net, but the teacher said it was 40–0 to Gemma. Soon Gemma stopped trying to hit the ball well because she won all the time anyway. They played six games and Gemma won all of them.

'Gemma, you can play with Robert now,' the teacher decided. 'You need someone who can play as well as you.'

'But I can't play well,' Gemma thought and she felt her face go red. Robert was a very good-looking boy from another class. She was usually too afraid to speak to him. She did *not* want to look stupid in front of Robert.

'He won't want to play with me,' she thought. 'I'm terrible and he's in the school team.'

She went to play with Robert and waited for him to hit the ball. He smiled at her, but not in a very friendly way. He hit the ball hard to Gemma. To Gemma's surprise she hit it back to him. It was out, but Robert ran for the ball anyway. He hit it, but it went up and came back down on his side.

'Well played,' he said. But he didn't look happy about it. Robert hit the ball harder and harder. Gemma wasn't playing well, but she was still winning.

'He's angry with me,' she thought. Every time Gemma made a mistake, Robert said she was winning.

They played for fifteen minutes until the class finished. Robert was red from running everywhere, but Gemma wasn't.

After the game Robert said something surprising.

'Maybe we can practise at the weekend. It looks like I need it!'

Robert wanted to play tennis with her! Gemma couldn't believe it.

'Who cares if I'm good at tennis or not?' she thought. 'I don't care why this is happening. Everyone will be so jealous that Robert and I are spending time together.'

'That would be great,' she answered, and smiled at Robert.

*   *   *

English was next and, while they were walking to class, Amy asked to see the phone again. Gemma showed it to her, but a boy tried to take it from her hands.

'Stop it!' shouted Amy. 'I was looking at that. It's *my* friend's phone!'

'What's going on here?' It was their English teacher.

'Gemma's got a new phone, Miss,' replied Amy.

'You know you musn't play with phones in class. Give it to me!' said the teacher.

Gemma suddenly remembered the old man's words.

'I'm sorry, Miss,' she argued. 'I can't give it to you. It's only for me!' But she stopped speaking when she saw the teacher's angry face. She gave her the phone. What else could she do?

The teacher was looking at the phone.

'Very funny,' she said. She read from the screen. '"Give me back to Gemma! This is Gemma's phone. It's not for teachers." Sorry, Gemma. Phones are also not for class.' She put it in her pocket.

'How did you do that?' Amy asked when they sat down.

'I didn't!' Gemma answered. 'I don't know how it knew—'

But Amy wasn't listening to her. She was looking at the teacher.

'Shhh!' Amy said. 'This is my favourite class.'

Gemma was surprised. 'But you hate English!'

'Everyone open your books at page ten,' said the teacher.

'Oh good! I love this book!' said one boy.

'Me too!' agreed another boy.

The teacher looked different in some way. Her clothes were really cool, her hair was a beautiful colour and her eyes were so blue.

'Actually,' Gemma thought. 'Amy's right. This is my favourite class too.'

The class was so interesting that Gemma forgot about the strange way the phone knew things.

At the end of the lesson, most of the students wanted to say thank you to the teacher.

'What a great class!' said one girl.

'Yes, thanks, Miss! Are we doing that book again next time?' said Amy.

The teacher smiled, but she looked very surprised.

'Oh … I'm happy you like it. We're doing this book until the holidays. The same as always.'

'You've got a really pretty smile, Miss,' said Gemma.

'Yes, Gemma. You can have your phone back! I know that's what you mean.'

'I forgot about the phone!' said Gemma and it was true.

The teacher gave it back to her.

'Don't forget to keep it in your bag in class, Gemma.'

Gemma put the phone in her bag. When she looked up she couldn't believe her eyes. The teacher's hair was grey again and her eyes weren't special at all. Even her clothes were different – brown and boring. Gemma thought she was starting to understand what was happening.

LOOKING BACK

1 Check your answers to *Looking forward* on page 15.

ACTIVITIES

2 Match the two parts of the sentences.

1 Gemma was surprised about the history test ☒f
2 Everyone wants to listen to Gemma's story ☐
3 Gemma's mum is pleased with her ☐
4 Gemma has to play tennis with Robert ☐
5 Gemma gives the English teacher her phone ☐
6 Gemma forgets about the phone ☐

a because they think it's amazing.
b because she can't use it in class.
c because she's playing so well.
d because the English lesson is so interesting.
e because she thinks she's working hard.
f because she got twenty out of twenty.

3 <u>Underline</u> the correct words in each sentence.

1 Gemma and Amy both love *history* / <u>*music*</u>.
2 Amy gets *twenty* / *six* out of twenty in the history test.
3 The history teacher is *happy* / *angry* with Gemma.
4 Gemma studies *a lot* / *a little* for the maths test.
5 *Robert* / *Amy* wants to play tennis with Gemma again.
6 *The teacher* / *Gemma* has the new phone in her pocket in the English lesson.
7 Everyone thinks the English lesson is really *interesting* / *boring*.

4 Who or what do the underlined words refer to?

> Gemma and Robert   Gemma and Amy   Gemma (x2)
> Amy   the history teacher (x2)

1 <u>They</u> were like each other in lots of ways. *Gemma and Amy*
2 <u>She</u> wasn't interested in things that happened long ago.

....

3 'Why did <u>you</u> give me twenty?' ....
4 Perhaps <u>he</u> was trying to be kind. ....
5 Why did <u>he</u> email her mother? ....
6 When <u>she</u> got her paper back she had an A. ....
7 'Maybe <u>we</u> can practise at the weekend.' ....

5 Answer the questions.

1 Why is Gemma surprised about getting twenty out of twenty in the history test?

....

2 Why doesn't Gemma do much maths homework?

....

3 What happens to the English teacher when she has the phone?

....

4 What happens to the English teacher when she gives the phone back to Gemma?

....

6 Tick (✓) what you think happens in Chapters 5, 6 and 7.

1 Gemma loses the phone. ☐
2 Gemma gets a new phone. ☐
3 Gemma enters a music competition. ☐

Chapter 5

I've lost it!

For the rest of the week, Gemma had a great time. In class, all the teachers thought she was the best student. Outside of class, everyone in school wanted to spend time with her. When she told a joke, everyone laughed. When she told a story, everyone listened. Every day people came up to her and said they loved her hair or her bag or her shoes.

'Can we come shopping with you on Saturday?' asked some of the girls.

'Of course!' said Gemma happily.

So, on Saturday, Gemma went to meet Amy and her new friends at the shops. She wore some old jeans and a T-shirt.

'Clothes aren't important anyway, are they?' she thought.

But when her friends arrived, they didn't like how she looked any more.

'Why are you wearing those jeans?' asked Amy.

'What happened to your hair?' asked another girl.

Gemma was surprised. She felt stupid, so she said quickly. 'It was a joke.' She waited for them to laugh as usual.

'They won't let you go into the shops like that,' said the girls. They laughed, but not in a nice way. 'We're going shopping by ourselves.'

Amy stayed, but Gemma still thought she was going to cry. She felt in her pocket for her phone. Then she had a terrible feeling in her stomach. The phone wasn't there!

'I had it when I left home!' she thought. 'How can I have lost it?' But the phone was gone.

Gemma thought about her new friends, her tennis playing, her school work. She thought about her English teacher and how beautiful she looked when she had the phone. Gemma knew it was all because of the phone. She couldn't pretend any longer. But she didn't want to think about what it meant. She just wanted the phone back. She remembered what the old man said to her mother in the shop: 'If she loses it, I can find it again.'

'We have to go to the phone shop, Amy!' Gemma said.

She ran to the shop with Amy behind her.

'Gemma!' the old man said. 'Have you lost your phone already?'

'Yes! Please say you can you find it!'

'Don't worry. It's only a phone,' he said. 'And I have it right here.'

'How did he find it so quickly?' Gemma thought in surprise. She decided that she didn't care. The important thing was that everything could be normal[10] again. Gemma forgot that nothing was normal any more.

Gemma felt better when she had the phone in her hand again. And she saw that she wasn't the only one who felt different.

'Gemma,' said Amy. 'Can we go shopping now? I want some jeans like yours.'

The man smiled. 'Are you happy with your phone?'

'Yes,' said Gemma in a strong voice. 'I'm happy. Very happy.'

'Good,' he said. 'Your report is going to be very interesting. I'm sure you're learning some important things, Gemma.'

Gemma didn't say anything. She was learning that she needed to keep the phone safe. That was all.

Chapter 6

We'll be famous

'Here you are, A again, Gemma,' said the teacher in the English class. She gave Gemma her homework. 'I can see you spent hours on this.'

Gemma took her homework and put it in her bag. She didn't look at it. It was her fifth A that week.

'Amy, see me after class,' the teacher said when she gave Amy hers.

Gemma felt bad when she saw Amy's D. She knew her A's didn't mean anything, but she couldn't tell Amy that.

'Oh no!' said Amy. 'Please can you help me next time?'

Gemma didn't know what to say. She felt terrible. There was no way she could help!

Most of her classes were like this now. She did well, but Amy still did badly. There was only one class they both did well in and that was music. Gemma was really good at playing the piano. She wasn't good at singing, but she didn't mind. She often played the piano while Amy sang – Amy had an amazing voice. Together they made a great team.

As Gemma walked to music, she felt someone's hand on her arm.

'How about playing tennis after school this afternoon?' said a boy's voice. It was Robert. Gemma tried to look cool, like she and Robert were old friends. Everyone could see Robert talking to her. She knew the other girls were watching.

'Oh. Tennis? Yes, sure!' she said. But Gemma was suddenly afraid. She felt in her pocket for her phone. She still had it, so there couldn't be any problem with tennis. But she checked every ten minutes, just to make sure.

In the music class Gemma couldn't think. She was too busy thinking about playing tennis with Robert. Luckily no one saw that she wasn't playing the piano as well as usual. She played and Amy sang. Gemma usually loved listening to Amy's wonderful, strong voice, but now she felt sick.

After music she went to change into her tennis clothes. 'What if the phone breaks?' she thought.

But there was nothing to worry about. She won again. They played until it was almost dark. Robert tried as hard as he could, but he could never win.

'Are you free on Friday?' he asked.

Gemma smiled. Of course she was free! Robert wanted to spend more time with her. This was great. Maybe next time they could go to a café with some of her friends.

'This is great practice for me,' he said. 'I need someone like you to play with to make my tennis better.'

Gemma tried to look pleased.

'More tennis?' she thought.

*   *   *

The next day, when Gemma arrived at the music class, the teacher, Mrs Hawkins, was putting a poster on the wall.

'I have some news for you all,' she said to the class. She smiled and pointed at the poster. 'I'm sure you all know the TV show, *Stars of Tomorrow.*'

Everyone knew it, of course. *Stars of Tomorrow* was one of the best shows on TV. It was a music competition[11] and the people who won became famous.

'Next week,' Mrs Hawkins said, 'there's going to be a competition at school. People from the show are coming here with their TV cameras. All of you can play and they'll choose the best. The people who win from our school will be in the competition in May with students from other schools. And they'll be on TV!'

Everyone in the class started talking at the same time.

'We can win that competition,' Gemma said to Amy.

It was true. Amy had the best voice in the school and Gemma was the best piano player. And, of course, she had the phone.

'I'm winning everything these days,' she thought. 'Why not this competition too? I won't even need to practise.'

* * *

The next day, when the teacher listened to them, she clapped her hands.

'You've learnt that song quickly!' she said. 'It has difficult piano music, Gemma, but you played beautifully. And Amy, you were wonderful as always.'

Gemma smiled. She knew her playing wasn't good.

'We're going to win!' Gemma said to Amy. She tried to forget how bad her playing was. Winning was the important thing.

'Let's start learning the other song,' said Amy.

'I can't,' Gemma said. 'I'm meeting Robert,' she said loudly, so the other girls could hear. 'You can practise without me, can't you?'

Amy looked down at the music.

'But we need to learn this new song. And I thought maybe you could help me with the maths homework later.'

'Sorry, Robert's waiting. We can do the maths another day,' Gemma said quickly. She felt bad because she knew she couldn't help Amy with her maths. She was already putting things in her bag, so she didn't have to see the look on Amy's face. She checked her pocket for the phone for the hundredth time that day.

Gemma didn't know why everything was so easy and so difficult at the same time. School and tennis were easy, but being a good friend was suddenly difficult. Everyone needed something from her. Amy needed her to play the piano, Robert wanted to practise tennis.

'What do I want?' she thought.

Chapter 7

What's wrong with Amy?

After tennis, Robert walked home with Gemma. He was easy to talk to and she was having fun now they weren't playing tennis. She told him about the music competition. But he already knew that she played the piano. She was surprised.

'I remember you from the end of year concert last summer,' he said. 'I wanted to play the piano like you when I was younger. I had a teacher, but I was terrible.'

'Well you're great at sports,' Gemma said. 'Everyone has something they're good at.'

Robert laughed.

'You're good at everything! Tennis, music, school. Is there anything you can't do?'

Gemma said nothing. What could she say? She knew she wasn't as special as he thought.

It was late when she got home. So Gemma ate her dinner, looked at her books and quickly did the most important homework. Then she felt tired. She looked at the piano.

'I can learn that new song tomorrow,' she thought. Ten minutes later, she fell asleep.

*   *   *

The next day, Gemma and Amy went to the music room at lunchtime to practise the new song. Mrs Hawkins was there. She was looking at some homework and listening to them play.

Gemma played the new song. She made lots of mistakes and it was terrible.

'You learnt that last night?' asked Amy.

'Yes, a bit. Sorry, it's not—'

'You know it already! After only one night?' Amy said. 'I can't remember all the words yet!'

Gemma wasn't surprised by this any more. It was still strange that no one could hear her mistakes. But she didn't say anything.

'You'll be OK. I'll help you,' said Gemma. 'We'll sing it together until you know the words.'

Usually Gemma didn't like singing in front of people because she knew she didn't have a good voice. But today only Amy and the teacher were listening. She sang the words quietly. She hated her voice – she thought it was ugly. She tried just to think about playing the piano music right. Amy sometimes forgot the words, so they did it again and again until she got it right. Gemma looked up from the piano and saw that Mrs Hawkins wasn't looking at homework now. She was listening to them and moving her feet to the music.

When Amy remembered all the words, Mrs Hawkins clapped her hands.

'Girls, that's amazing! Your two voices are beautiful together.'

'Yes,' Amy said slowly. 'I didn't know you could sing like that, Gemma.'

'But I was terrible!' Gemma said. 'I was only helping you learn the words. I can't sing at all!'

'You don't need to pretend, Gemma,' Mrs Hawkins said. 'Sing together in the competition if you want to win.'

Amy smiled, but only with her mouth. She didn't look at Gemma.

'I think we've practised enough. I'm going to lunch,' Amy said.

She left without waiting for Gemma. They weren't spending much time together these days.

Gemma thought about staying in the music room to practise. But without Amy it wasn't much fun.

'I don't need to practise anyway!' Gemma remembered. The phone meant she never needed to work hard for anything ever again.

LOOKING BACK

1 Check your answers to *Looking forward* on page 29.

ACTIVITIES

2 Put the sentences in order.
1 Mrs Hawkins tells the class about the music competition. ☐
2 Gemma goes shopping with Amy and some other girls. ☐1
3 Robert and Gemma play tennis again. ☐
4 Gemma and Amy go to the phone shop. ☐
5 Amy tells Gemma she likes her jeans. ☐
6 Gemma and Amy practise for the music competition. ☐
7 Gemma can't find her phone. ☐
8 Gemma's friends don't like how she looks. ☐

3 Are the sentences true (*T*) or false (*F*)?
1 Gemma does really well at school. ☐T
2 The old man in the shop has got Gemma's phone. ☐
3 Gemma wants to have a different phone. ☐
4 Gemma helps Amy with her school work. ☐
5 Gemma isn't usually good at singing. ☐
6 Gemma likes playing tennis with Robert. ☐
7 The winners of the music competition will be on TV. ☐
8 Gemma is going to practise a lot for the music competition. ☐

4 Complete the sentences with the names from the box.

> Gemma's new friends   the old man   Amy (x3)
> Gemma (x3)

1 .... want to go shopping by themselves.
2 .... finds Gemma's phone.
3 .... gets a D for the English homework.
4 .... plays the piano really well.
5 .... and .... make a great team.
6 .... helps .... learn the new song.

5 Answer the questions.

1 Why don't Gemma's new friends want to go shopping with her when they see her?

....

2 Why does Amy say she likes Gemma's jeans?

....

3 Why can't Gemma help Amy with her work?

....

4 Why doesn't Gemma practise the piano at home?

....

LOOKING FORWARD

6 Tick (✓) what you think happens in the last three chapters.

1 Gemma and Amy stop being friends. ☐
2 Gemma loses the phone again. ☐
3 Gemma plays in the music competition. ☐

Chapter 8

This isn't fun any more

Gemma spent the evening reading magazines about famous people. She looked at their beautiful clothes and their amazing holidays and she dreamed that she lived like them. She thought about arriving at a top restaurant with hundreds of people and photographers outside.

'What will I wear to the competition?' she thought suddenly. So she spent the rest of the evening choosing the right clothes and doing her hair. She called Amy to ask what she wanted to wear. But there was no answer.

Gemma's homework books stayed in her bag and she didn't practise for the competition at all.

* * *

At school the next day, Amy left every class quickly without waiting. Amy didn't want to talk to her, Gemma knew. It wasn't a nice feeling.

At lunchtime Gemma was walking past the music room. She stopped when she heard someone singing. It was Amy.

'Why is Amy practising without me?' Gemma thought, sad again that Amy didn't want to spend time with her.

She listened at the door. Amy really did have a very beautiful voice.

For a minute Gemma felt angry. 'It's not fair!' she thought. 'I want to hear my voice the way everyone else can hear it.'

'That's great, Amy!' Gemma heard Mrs Hawkins say.

'But it's not as good as Gemma, is it?' said Amy.

'Don't think like that!' said Mrs Hawkins. 'You're both great, but your voices are different. Just practise and do your best. That's all anyone can do.'

'I've always loved singing, but now I feel I'm not good enough. Gemma didn't practise, but she sings amazingly now,' said Amy.

'You *are* good enough, but you have to work hard too. Gemma probably practises every night and you just don't know about it.'

Gemma didn't want to listen any more. Mrs Hawkins was wrong. Gemma didn't practise singing or even the piano now.

'Am I enjoying playing and singing?' she thought as she walked away. 'I can't hear that my voice is amazing when I sing.'

She took out her phone and started to send a message to Amy. She wanted to say something to make Amy feel better. But she didn't know what to write.

Two boys walked past and she saw them looking at her phone.

'That's the phone I told you about,' one of the boys told his friend.

Gemma quickly put the phone in her pocket.

'It's just a phone!' she said loudly.

The boys both laughed.

'You've got to hear the story of how she got the phone,' said the boy. 'It's so cool.'

Gemma was so bored of telling this stupid story! It *wasn't* cool. She wasn't enjoying the phone at all now. It was like singing and playing the piano and playing tennis. She wasn't even enjoying getting A's all the time. Nothing was special for her, only for other people.

'Spending time with Robert is fun,' she thought. But was it? They always played tennis and that was all he cared about.

Gemma didn't know what to think. It was making her tired.

*   *   *

In English Gemma sat next to Amy.

'Do you want to practise our song after school?' asked Gemma at the end of the lesson.

'I'm sure you've got better things to do,' said Amy. 'Robert is probably waiting for you to play tennis.'

'I can play later!' said Gemma quickly.

'Well, I'm busy,' said Amy.

'Oh, OK,' said Gemma. But she didn't feel OK. 'What about at the weekend? The competition is on Monday, so we have to practise.'

'Why do you want me to do so much practice?' asked Amy. 'You don't need to practise.'

'I just wanted to practise together too,' Gemma said carefully.

'To see if I'm good enough, you mean,' said Amy angrily.

'No—' Gemma started to say. But Amy just walked away.

Chapter 9

Who wants normal?

Gemma sent Amy messages all morning on Saturday, but there was no reply. She hoped Amy was practising. The only message Gemma got was from the phone.

'It's time to give your report, Gemma,' it said. How did the phone know that?

'I can ask the old man,' Gemma thought as she went to the shop.

'It's great to see you again, Gemma,' said the old man. He was smiling warmly. 'Have you come to tell me about your phone?'

'Yes,' Gemma said. She didn't know how much to say about the strange phone.

'The phone makers will be very happy to hear what you think,' the man said. He took out a piece of paper and a pen.

Gemma felt something dancing in her stomach. It wasn't a nice feeling.

'Now,' the old man said. 'Tell me about the phone and I'll write down what you say.'

'Well,' began Gemma. 'It … it … it worked OK.'

'Which features did you like best?' he asked.

Gemma couldn't think of anything to say. She couldn't say it made her beautiful and good at everything.

'Actually, I didn't find anything very special about it.' The dancing in her stomach got faster.

The old man wrote as she was speaking.

'Oh?'

Gemma took the phone out of her pocket and looked at it. Now that the first words were out of her mouth, it was easier to say more.

'You know what one amazing thing was? Everyone else thought it was great, but not me.'

'Well, you wanted a phone that everyone thinks is cool,' the man said.

'Yes,' said Gemma. 'I did want that. Now I don't know.' She remembered how everyone thought she was cool and funny and good at everything. 'I can't see things the way everyone else sees them.'

'If the phone isn't special for you, then maybe you'd like a different phone?' the man said.

'No!' Gemma almost shouted. She closed her hand around the phone. She suddenly felt very afraid that the man wanted to take it away from her. 'I mean, no thank you. This is the phone I want. I'm happy. I am!'

'You don't look very happy to me,' he said kindly. 'And you didn't look very happy the last time I saw you. How others see us is always different from how we see ourselves.'

Gemma didn't want to think about it any more. She changed the conversation.

'How does the phone know things?' she asked.

'Things like what?' he answered her.

'It knew it was time to give my report. It knows who I am!'

'Do you know who you are, Gemma?' the man asked.

Gemma didn't know any more. 'Am I the person other people see?' she asked herself. 'Am I the amazing student, the tennis player, the singer? Is that me?'

She knew it wasn't. But the real Gemma didn't sing well enough to win the competition and that was the important thing. Wasn't it? She was tired of thinking about it.

'There's a music competition at our school on Monday,' she said suddenly. 'It's for *Stars of Tomorrow*. My friend Amy sings and we're going to win! You'll see us on TV!'

'And what do you do? Do you sing or play something?' he asked.

'I play the piano. I can't sing well at all, but everyone thinks I can now!'

'Gemma, Gemma,' he said sadly. 'If singing makes you happy, then it's not important what everyone else thinks. Is Amy happy when she sings?'

Gemma thought about when Amy was talking to the music teacher. Her friend loved singing before, but Amy wasn't enjoying it now, was she?

But she didn't say that. She said, 'Amy will be happy when we win the competition. We're going to be famous!'

The man smiled.

'Good luck[12] to you and Amy then. Now, before you go, please can I see the phone again?'

Gemma gave him her phone. He looked at it carefully and turned it over to look at the back.

He smiled again. 'Things will probably go back to normal now.'

'Normal?' Gemma thought. 'Who wants normal? We're going to win that competition and then we'll be on TV!'

* * *

The next day was Sunday. Gemma usually did something with Amy on Sundays. But when she called Amy there was no answer. Gemma didn't need to practise. And without her friend practising wasn't fun any more – without Amy the weekend wasn't fun at all. So when Robert called and invited Gemma to the park near his house for more tennis she agreed.

But things were very different today. Gemma had the phone in her pocket and she was playing the same as usual. But something was wrong. When she hit the ball it went out. When Robert hit the ball it was usually in and she couldn't hit it back. This was how she played before she had the phone. But Robert didn't mind that she was playing badly.

'I've won two games!' Robert said happily. 'Are you pretending to play badly to make me feel good?' He laughed.

Gemma was too tired to reply.

'I have to sit down,' Gemma said, drying her face with her T-shirt. 'I'm really hot.'

'Are you sure you're OK?' Robert asked. 'Maybe you're ill. Let's go to my house and get a drink.'

Gemma wasn't ill, she just didn't usually do a lot of sport. When she played tennis with Robert before, she didn't work very hard at all.

They went to Robert's house and sat in the living room and drank water.

'You've got a piano!' she said when she saw the piano in the corner of the room.

Robert made a face.

'Yes, everyone in our family plays except me.'

'It's a beautiful piano. I've never played one like that before,' Gemma said.

'Would you like to play it?' he asked. 'I'd love to hear you play something.'

'Do you want to hear the music we're going to do in the competition?' she asked.

Gemma closed her eyes and played the music. She made a lot of mistakes. She wasn't making music; it was noise and she hated hearing herself.

'Lucky Robert,' she thought. 'He probably thinks it's amazing.'

Robert listened kindly until she stopped.

'Maybe you really are ill, Gemma,' he joked. 'That was as bad as your tennis!'

Gemma was surprised. 'He's the first person to hear my mistakes,' she thought. She didn't need to check her pocket. She knew the phone was there, but she had a terrible feeling it wasn't working any more. 'This is it,' she thought. 'Now he's not going to like me.'

'Maybe you need to sing too, to help you remember the music,' Robert said. He was trying to help.

Gemma's mouth was suddenly dry. 'I can't really sing you know,' she said.

'Yes, you can,' he said. 'I heard you practising with Amy last week. You're an amazing singer. Go on, don't be afraid!'

Gemma started playing again. When she opened her mouth to sing, out came the ugly noises and terrible voice she always sang with. She saw Robert's face and stopped.

Robert tried to be kind.

'You're just tired from the tennis or ...' Then he started laughing. 'Oh, I see! It's a joke!'

'No,' Gemma said quietly. 'That's my normal voice.'

She suddenly remembered the last thing the old man in the shop said yesterday. 'Things will probably go back to normal now.'

Normal? Normally she was bad at tennis. Normally she couldn't sing and she didn't get A's in class without spending hours on her homework. Normally people didn't tell her how beautiful she was all the time or laugh at all her jokes. Normally she needed to practise the piano to be good.

'Robert, you're going to need a new tennis partner!' She stood up suddenly. 'I have to go!' And she ran out of the house before he could say anything.

Chapter 10

Can we win?

When she got home Gemma tried calling Amy again, but Amy still wasn't answering her phone. 'I hope she's practising,' Gemma thought. 'But now it's me that needs to practise. I hope I have enough time!'

Gemma spent the rest of the day playing the piano. She wanted to be as good as she could be, so she practised for hours. But she didn't sing. 'I don't need to practise that,' she thought happily.

*　　*　　*

Gemma sneezed[13] loudly.

'Are you OK, Gemma?' asked Mrs Hawkins in the music class on Monday morning.

'I'm ill,' said Gemma in a strange, dry voice. She sneezed three more times.

'Oh no!' said one of the students. 'What about the competition?'

Gemma could see that Amy was listening to their conversation.

'I'm lucky that I'm with Amy ...' said Gemma.

She looked at Amy again, but Amy was looking somewhere else.

'I hope this works,' Gemma thought and sneezed again loudly.

After class, Gemma waited for Amy. 'Do you want to have lunch together?' she asked.

'I'm not sure,' Amy said.

Gemma felt bad. Amy didn't want to do anything with her.

But then Amy smiled. 'We need to practise, don't you think?' she said. Gemma smiled back and put her arms round her friend.

'I'm so happy you said that! I practised the piano for hours yesterday. And I know you'll be amazing. We can't lose!'

'Get off!' Amy laughed. She moved away. 'I don't want to catch your cold!'

'Oh yes,' said Gemma. She laughed and pretended to sneeze again. 'I forgot about my terrible cold!'

*   *   *

Everybody in the school came to watch the competition. The TV cameras were there and people were trying to stand where the cameras could see them.

While Gemma was waiting with Amy, Robert came to find her.

'Good luck! Don't forget me when you're famous!' he said.

But there was no time to answer.

'Next it's Gemma and Amy!' said the man from *Stars of Tomorrow* to the camera.

Gemma was afraid when she walked in front of the cameras and sat down at the piano. But when Amy started singing Gemma forgot about the cameras and tried to play her best. She wanted to play well for her friend. Amy sang better than ever before and Gemma played beautifully. She felt she was flying with the music.

After they finished, she and Amy stood hand in hand while everyone in the school clapped. She saw Robert and her mother smiling happily.

'Do you think we'll win?' asked Amy.

'I already feel like we've won,' said Gemma. And it was true. People were clapping for *her*, not the phone. Without the phone she wasn't good at everything, but she had everything she wanted.

'If this is normal,' she thought as she looked at the people smiling and clapping, 'then normal is amazing!'

LOOKING BACK

1   Check your answers to *Looking forward* on page 43.

ACTIVITIES

2   Put the sentences in order.

1   Gemma plays the piano and sings for Robert. ☐

2   Gemma pretends to have a cold. ☐

3   Gemma goes back to the phone shop. ☐1

4   The old man looks at Gemma's phone. ☐

5   Gemma goes to Robert's house. ☐

6   Gemma and Amy do the music competition. ☐

7   Gemma plays tennis badly. ☐

8   Gemma practises the piano for hours. ☐

3   Match the two parts of the sentences.

1   Amy is sad ☐c

2   Gemma is angry ☐

3   Gemma goes to the phone shop ☐

4   Gemma is afraid in the phone shop ☐

5   On Sunday Gemma gets tired playing tennis ☐

6   Gemma practises the piano a lot on Sunday ☐

a   because she thinks the old man is going to take the phone.

b   because she wants to do well in the competition.

c   because she thinks her voice isn't as good as Gemma's.

d   because she can't hear her voice the way other people can.

e   because she doesn't usually have to work hard.

f   because she gets a message on her phone.

4 Are the sentences true (*T*) or false (*F*)?

1 Gemma hears Amy practising at school without her. ☐T

2 Mrs Hawkins thinks Gemma practises a lot. ☐

3 The old man in the shop does something to Gemma's phone. ☐

4 At the weekend Gemma speaks to Amy on the phone. ☐

5 Gemma spends Sunday with Amy. ☐

6 When they play tennis, Robert thinks Gemma is ill. ☐

7 On Monday, Gemma has a really bad cold. ☐

8 At the competition Gemma plays really badly. ☐

5 Answer the questions.

1 Why doesn't Gemma think the phone is great any more?

....

2 Why does Gemma start to play tennis badly?

....

3 Why doesn't Gemma need to practise her singing?

....

4 Why does Gemma pretend to have a cold?

....

5 Do you think Gemma wants to win the competition? Why or why not?

....

Glossary

[1]**pretend** (page 6) *verb*   to make other people think something is true when it's not

[2]**surprised** (page 7) *adjective*   you feel surprised about things that are new or you didn't know before

[3]**report** (page 8) *noun*   something you write to give information about something

[4]**jealous** (page 8) *adjective*   you feel jealous when you really want something someone else has got

[5]**surprise** (page 9) *noun*   something like a present or a party that you didn't know about before it happened

[6]**amazing** (page 10) *adjective*   very good, great, wonderful

[7]**clap** (page 17) *verb*   to put your hands together to make a sound when you think something is really good

[8]**suddenly** (page 20) *adverb*   something happens suddenly if it happens very quickly and you didn't know it was going to happen

[9]**hit** (page 13) *verb*   to touch two things together quickly; you hit the ball in tennis, golf and cricket

[10]**normal** (page 32) *adjective*   usual, not different

[11]**competition** (page 36) *noun*   something someone can win and other people can lose; usually you win a prize

[12]**Good luck** (page 51) *expression*   you say this when someone is going to do a competition or something difficult – it means you hope they'll be lucky

[13]**sneeze** (page 56) *verb*   you sneeze through your nose, for example when you have a cold